Jill Silverthorne

D1633579

A Cobweb Covered Conspiracy

DayOne

© Day One Publications 2015

First printed 2015

ISBN 978-1-84625-442-0

All Scripture quotations are from the **New International Version** 1984
Copyright © 1973, 1978, 1984

Published by Day One Publications
Ryelands Road, Leominster, HR6 8NZ

TEL 01568 613 740 FAX 01568 611 473

email—sales@dayone.co.uk

UK web site—www.dayone.co.uk

Designed by **documen**
Printed by TJ International

Dedication

For everyone who has been bullied—and
for anyone who helped them.

Chapter one

I'll never forget the day he told me the story. It was the day I stabbed myself—the day the war with Joe Fuller began. Well OK, not really. That started long before the stabbing—and it would only end when one of us was utterly defeated.

A Tuesday it was, and it started pretty much the same as usual. I raced down the four flights of stairs from our flat and checked my watch. Seven minutes. I'd have to shift it. Six minutes and forty seconds it took to get to school—as long as the lights were on red. If not, anything up to seven and a half. I started to run.

As I turned the corner, the traffic lights were reflecting in the Pizza Plaza window. Red. I slowed down, but I shouldn't have been so stupid. The lights only went and changed on me, and there wasn't a gap in the traffic. 'C'mon, c'mon!' I said under my breath, watching the seconds fade on my watch. Amber. Red.

I pelted across the road into Edgar Street, knowing all the time it was hopeless. As I reached the green *Plowright Academy for Boys* sign, I heard a magpie laugh somewhere in the distance and the bell went for the start of school. Late again! Fuming, I slowed to a walk and took my tie out of my pocket.

'Good *afternoon*,' came a sarcastic voice.

I groaned. 'Ansome Anselm, the Deputy Head, was at the gate, loving his first job of the day: bawling out late arrivers.

I concentrated on knotting my tie and getting my two eagles' logo to show—anything rather than look at him. 'Sorry sir. It was the traffic lights.'

He crouched a bit to get in my face, and my glasses steamed up with his coffee breath. I stepped back. 'Get out of bed earlier then. Some boys actually arrive every day *before* the bell goes. Wouldn't it be nice to witness that phe-no-men-on?'

I didn't get what he was going on about, so I shrugged my shoulders. 'Ansome scanned his clipboard.

'First late of the week. Not bad for a *Tuesday*, Michael.' And he laughed his stupid laugh somewhere in the back of his throat.

'Martin, sir.' 'Ansome looked up. 'My name's Martin, not Michael.'

'Martin, Michael. I don't care what your name is when you're late. One more this week and you know what that means?'

Why did he always have to shout? 'Yes sir.'

'Don't mumble. What does it mean?

'A detention, sir.'

'Well done.' He was so patronising, but in fact he looked like an overgrown penguin, trying to clap and balance his clipboard at the same time. If I wasn't so scared of him, I would have laughed. He wrote my name down and shooed me off to registration.

'Sorry I'm late, Miss.' I slid into my seat beside Joe. Joe Fuller.

'Four Eyes!' He punched me in the arm as I sat down. 'Did you get caught? Man, you're rubbish.' I chewed my lip and said nothing.

When registration was over, Miss Lancelot asked me to take a message to the office. It was fine until the others left, and she got that 'There's something I need to say to you' look on her face. 'Don't get another detention will you, Martin? You were always on time last year. What's changed?'

'Dunno, Miss.' I felt myself going red. She meant well, I know, but she wouldn't believe me if I told her the truth. I turned to go, but she stopped me.

'Not so fast, Martin. Are you staying up late playing on the computer?'

Now I know it was a lie, but it got me out of an awkward situation. 'Probably, Miss. I'll make sure I'm off earlier.' Before she could say any more, I was gone.

The day didn't get any better. In Geography, Joe was messing around, but Mr Carter shouted at me for it. Joe, of course, said nothing, and I took the blame. As usual.

Behind the Art rooms at lunchtime, Joe took the sunny end of the bench and put his bag down next to him. Now Joe's not small, if you know what I mean, and there wasn't room for me with him *and* his bag.

'Budge up,' I said. I shouldn't have bothered. He totally ignored me and opened his crisps. I gave up, perched on the arm of the bench, and shivered. It was cold out of the sun. I started on my sandwich while Joe finished his crisps, dropped the packet and rubbed his hands on his trousers. Then he took a can out of his bag, pulled the ring and pointed it at me. The hissy fizz told me it had been rolling around all morning and a fountain shot in my direction.

'Hey! Watch out!' I wiped a long dribble of froth from my blazer.

Joe laughed, and made the 'L' sign. After a swig and an almighty burp, he laughed again. 'Los-er. All you need now is to show yourself up in rugby this afternoon.'

I groaned. Rugby was a nightmare. When I played, I had to take my glasses off, but then everything was blurry. The week before had been a disaster. Mr Hogarth had called me a knock-kneed giraffe or something like that. Much as I hated him for it—and everyone for laughing—I know I'd have joined in too if he'd said it about anyone else.

I put my sandwich down. I didn't feel hungry any more.

Joe was watching me with his piggy little eyes. 'Pull a sicky. They never check.'

My stomach was feeling butterfly-ey. And come to think of it, my head was beginning to ache too. I put my lunchbox in my bag and stood up. 'Yeah. Perhaps I'll go to the first aid room.'

Joe aimed a kick at a sparrow pecking round his feet. 'So I can have your kit then.'

A set-up. Once again. How on earth didn't I see it coming? I was mad. 'You've forgotten your stuff, haven't you? Well, mine's too small for you, *Fuller*, so forget that.' As soon as I said it, I knew I shouldn't have. He could call me names as much as he wanted, but me do it back? No way!

I turned and winced as Joe trod on the heel of my shoe, his toe biting into my ankle. He stood up and I felt his warm breath, like 'Ansome's, on the back of my neck. He pressed his foot in harder and I winced. 'Don't you *ever* call me that, Four Eyes. Now give me your kit.'

'It's in the form room,' I heard myself say. And I hated myself for it.

Mrs Naismith in the first aid room pulled a face. 'So what's your story?' She always took some persuading. 'Sit down over there. We'll see what you're like in half an hour.'

It was over an hour before I woke up. My neck ached and Mrs Naismith looked across as I rubbed it. 'Mmm. Perhaps you are sickening for something.' She checked the clock above her desk. There were twenty-five minutes until the end of the day.

'I could do with some fresh air,' I said. 'And it's PE now. Can I go up to the field?'

She nodded.

Chapter two

I slung my bag behind the posts and watched the boys running towards me. It was then that I caught sight of Joe. He was at the back as usual, puffing and panting, and my top was riding up, showing his fat rolls to perfection. I put my hand over my mouth so he couldn't see me laughing.

The ball went back to Joe and he put his head down for a charge. 'Go, Fuller!' someone shouted, but suddenly he dropped the ball and stood stock still, wrapping his arms around himself.

'You winded?' Mr Hogarth shouted.

Joe made his way to the sideline and I walked over. He held up his arm and showed me what was wrong. He'd only gone and ripped my shirt: the sleeve was hanging right off! I felt sick. Mum would be furious: she'd saved for ages for my uniform.

When his back was turned in the changing rooms, I kicked a clod of mud at Joe. From somewhere, chanting started up. 'Flabby Fuller's too fat for his kit!' Seb Phillips snatched my dirty green shirt from the floor and threw it over Joe's head.

'No!' I yelled, but no one took any notice. As usual.

'Thompson, to you!' Joe stretched for it and the others laughed at his belly wobbling. Andy Thompson caught it and threw it to Webster.

'Come and get it,' called Shaun. Joe lunged, but Shaun was too quick. He jumped onto the bench and dangled it over his head. 'Come and get your *little* shirt, Fuller!' Joe finally snatched it from him, and threw it as hard as he could. Why, oh why, did it have to be right then that Mr Hogarth walked in? The room fell silent as he slowly untangled the flying shirt from his head, and wiped mud from his cheek. 'Whose is this?' he asked in a very low voice. My mouth went dry. He turned the collar over, read the name tag and eyeballed me. 'Martin Morris. Outside. Now!'

When I got home, I didn't bother putting the lights on. I sat on the sofa with Becker. He's my Jack Russell and everything's OK when he's around. My phone buzzed. I took it out and squinted at the square of light. A text. From Joe. I pressed 'Delete' without reading it. 'C'mon Becker.' I stood up. 'This is no good, is it?'

On Tuesdays, I made the tea. Mum finished work at half five and Grampa came home just before that. I helped myself to a biscuit, then took the meat out of the fridge. The chicken portions slithered from the tray onto the chopping board and I took the biggest knife from the block. I raised it above my head in both hands and brought it down hard, skewering the poor chicken. Excalibur! I have a good imagination, or so my Grampa says. The chopping board chinked in protest as I brought the knife down again and again, until I got cramp and pointed the blade at the mangled heap: 'Don't mess with me, Flabby Fuller.'

I flexed my hand to get rid of the cramp, took my glasses off, and started on the onion. It was a strong one. I squeezed my eyes to stop the tears, but I had to force them open as my finger started to sting. Red. I tried again. A steady drip of red to the lino. I grabbed the tea-towel, clamped my finger and felt myself swaying. I didn't remember any more until I heard ringing and Becker yapping.

'Martin! Martin!' The flap on the letter-box dropped and the ringing started again.

'I'm coming. Be with you. Yeah, coming.' I didn't really know what I was saying, and when I stood up, I felt sick. Then I remembered my hand. I steadied myself on the walls, and it wasn't until the next day I saw the rusty smears I'd left behind.

'Are you alright, Martin?' Grampa was worried when I opened the door. Amanda, the day centre bus driver, was with him. 'Go on in, Mr Skerritt,' she said.

Grampa was trying to unzip his coat. 'Can you help him?' I said, and raised my hand with the blood stained tea-towel over it. Amanda pulled a face. When she'd settled Grampa in the living room with Becker, she came back. 'So what have you been up to?'

My head was clearing and I opened the kitchen door. A trail of blood ran across the floor and a red stained onion sat half-chopped next to the butchered meat.

'What on earth ...?' she said.

'Killer chicken.' I managed a smile.

'Well that's the end of your cooking for today, young man. Now, where's your first aid kit?'

Mum arrived out of breath as Amanda was patching me up. 'Is Dad OK?' she shouted as she let herself in. I wondered how she knew something was wrong, but then I remembered: the day centre bus was still outside.

'He's fine,' said Amanda as Mum came into the kitchen. 'This one's the problem.'

'Sorry about tea,' I said, holding up my hand.

After Amanda had gone, Mum set to and sorted out our tea. It was half seven before we sat down, and we were starving. Just as we were about to eat, the phone went. Mum rolled her eyes as she picked it up.

'Joe!' she said. It was ages until she said anything else, but she locked her eyes on me. 'No,' she said eventually, 'you were right to tell me, Joe. I'm sorry. Where would I be without you, eh? Bye for now.'

'Something wrong?' I asked.

Mum put her tray on the settee. 'You tell me. Today. Rugby?'

'Oh that!' I'd forgotten all about PE with the stabbing.

'Oh yes: that,' she said. 'And you thought you could get away with it?'

'Away with ...?' What was she talking about?

'Pretending you'd given your shirt to Joe and saying he'd split it, when you'd ripped it before the lesson to get out of doing rugby.'

My jaw dropped. 'But Mum ...'

Her voice rose. 'Don't you *but Mum* me!'

Grampa's pretty deaf, but even he heard. He touched his hearing aid and it squealed. 'Is everything alright?'

'Fine,' my mum snapped. She waited for him to go back to his dinner. 'Go and get your rugby shirt out of your bag and show me it isn't ripped. I might believe you then.'

'But ...'

She gave me 'that' look and I knew I was doomed. When I came back, she snatched the shirt from me, and the last few green threads gave way. Mum was left holding the sleeve and I had the rest.

Even Grampa could tell that something was wrong. 'Leticia,' he said. 'Leticia!' But she took no notice.

She shook the sleeve in my face. 'How d'you expect me to pay for another one? You tell me that!'

'Joe's lying, Mum. He's lying.'

'So why are you in detention if Joe's lying? He wouldn't lie: he's been brought up too well for that. You're the liar, Martin Morris.'

I couldn't think of anything else to say—and neither could she. She threw the sleeve at me. 'Bin it. I've had enough.'

It was hopeless. I couldn't explain the detentions to her. After all, they fitted Joe's story perfectly, didn't they? He knew what he was doing—as usual—and I was set up yet again.

When I came back from the bin, I could hear Mum talking to Grampa, 'He's a liar, just like his father. And look where he ended up.'

Chapter three

Dad? I hadn't been allowed to talk about him, since he'd ... gone away.

A lump in my throat hardened and my finger throbbed. I didn't wait to hear any more. I went to the bedroom I shared with Grampa, lay on my bed and listened to the cars—my usual trick to distract myself. When I was little, I counted how many went past. Then I learnt to tell them apart by their engines. A Focus, a van of some sort, and a Jag. Then a pause: the lights must have changed. A diesel Avensis and a Renault Espace came through. I started to doze off.

It only seemed like minutes later when the light snapped on. I squinted in the brightness. Mum. She didn't even bother to ask about my finger. 'It's after ten. Get up and keep your Grampa company.'

Mum works all the shifts she can to keep us, and I have to look after Grampa when she's not there. That's the deal. Simple. He hasn't slept brilliantly since his fall, and I have to stay up with him until he's ready for bed. And that's rarely before midnight. But I can't tell that to Miss Lancelot, can I?

Grampa looked serious when I went into the living room. 'You've upset your mother.' I sat down on the settee and tapped it with my good hand. Becker jumped up. He only does that when Mum isn't there. 'I don't like to see my girl angry.'

'Grampa, I didn't lie.'

He stared at me long and hard. Then he shook his head. 'No, I don't think you did.' That made me feel better. 'But your ma does,' he continued, 'and that's the problem.' We sat in silence for a while and Grampa stared at my bandage. 'How's your finger?'

'Sore.'

'I thought so.' He paused for a moment and winked. 'It reminds me of a story from home I could tell you.'

I smiled.

Grampa's nearly eighty—tall and thin and wrinkled like a walnut. One of my earliest memories is tracing the creases in his face. 'Why are you all line-y, Grampa?' I'd asked.

'They're wisdom lines!' Then he put on his West Indian voice: 'Mih's a book full ah wis-dahm!'

Grampa and Grandma came to England in 1955. But home wasn't the shared house where they first lived, or the brand new council house where they'd had my mum. And it definitely wasn't Flat 4c Poplar Square. Home was Trinidad.

He's a great story-teller, my Grampa, and I think I get my imagination from him. When I was little, I'd fall asleep to his gravelly voice, West Indian sunshine on my skin and the noise of the sea in my ears.

Grampa told stories when anyone would listen and this was as good a time as any. He sat forward in his chair and made a cathedral with his hands.

'There was once a spider called Anancy ...' Becker twitched in his sleep. Grampa frowned. 'I can't remember like I used to.' He thought for a minute. 'Ah yes. It was a hot, hot day and Anancy was fed up of the sun. He'd spun webs all morning and it was too hot to carry on, so he settled back to doze in the shade of a banyan tree.' Grampa's voice slowed. 'Anancy's eyes grew heavy.

'Suddenly, there was a plop. Anancy opened one eye. He heard another plop, then another, then another. "Is it rain?" he thought. He opened both eyes and looked up. *Plop*—a large stone landed on the soil right beside him. "Hey!"' he called, and a screeching laugh in the tree gave Monkey away.

'Monkey was eating mango and hailing the stones down on Anancy.' Grampa jiggled his eyebrows. '"Hey Monkey," called Anancy. "What d'you think you're doing?"

"Mang-o," shouted Monkey.'

I laughed. Grampa's voices were magic, and Monkey was definitely the best.

'"Ah found mih a mango!" And another stone plopped on the soil.

'Anancy was furious. And he was thirsty. Nothing would be nicer than a soft, juicy mango. "Remember, Monkey, it's polite to share."

'Now Monkey remembered the last time he'd shared with Anancy. He'd ended up with nothing. "Why is yuh tellin mih, Spider? Ah is no nincompoop. Yuh go fin' yuh own mango!"

'Anancy was angry, but he said nothing. He moved to the other side of the tree and he thought. And he thought.

19

And he thought. And the mango stones kept raining over his head.

'Suddenly, Monkey let out a screech. "Aye-yah-yie! Aye-yah-yie!" There was a silence, followed by more shouting. "Yuh der, Anancy? Mih need yuh help."

'But Anancy held his peace.

'Monkey shrieked louder, and the hummingbird and the frigatebird and the bananaquit flew past to see what was happening. "Ah cut mihself. Ah is bleedin to death! Get help, quick!" And the birds flew off. Monkey screeched louder and louder. Anancy yawned and stretched.'

Grampa had that faraway look in his eyes. He wasn't with me anymore. He was back in Trinidad.

'"Do you need some help, Monkey?"

"Anancy. Dat yuh?"

"Yes, Monkey."

"Up here. Quick, Anancy."

'Anancy scrambled up the tree trunk to the fork where Monkey was sitting. He'd cut his paw on a mango stone. Anancy smiled to himself. "My, my. That's bad, Monkey. That's a lot of blood, a lot of blood. But I can help, if you'll let me."

'Monkey looked suspicious. But he needed his paw to swing and to eat mango. "Alright Anancy. Wha' yuh do?"

'Anancy edged closer. "I'll show you. But first, will you repay me with one tiny little mango?"

'Monkey was desperate. "A course Anancy: but only wahn. Now mend mih paw."

'Anancy bowed and began to spin his web.

"Give me your paw," said Anancy after a few minutes. "My web will mend the cut."

'Monkey was puzzled, but he held out his paw. Anancy threaded his web round and round, and sure enough, the bleeding slowed. At first Monkey didn't notice Anancy winding the web further up his arm. When he did, Anancy said, "A precaution, Monkey, just a precaution. Sit very still."

'Soon Monkey's arm and his shoulder and his back were covered in Anancy's web. "This will make sure you don't bleed any more," said Anancy. "Only a few more winds." Monkey sighed, but he sat as still as he could, and Anancy wound the web around the branch of the tree. "There!" said Anancy, "How does that feel?"

'Monkey tried to stretch, but he couldn't. And Monkey tried to stand, but he couldn't. He was stuck in Anancy's web! Anancy inched along the branch and rolled a mango from Monkey's heap to the ground. "One for me!" he said. "And another. And another. All for me!"

'Monkey was furious. He struggled and struggled, but he couldn't move. And all his mangoes soon disappeared.

"The bleeding's stopped, Monkey," said Anancy as he skipped past him along the branch. "It's a good sign!"

'Monkey screeched as Anancy made his way down the tree and rolled the mangoes to his house. When the frigatebird and the bananaquit and the hummingbird returned, they freed Monkey. But Anancy was nowhere to be found.'

Grampa sat back in his chair and folded his arms.

I tried to clap with my bandaged hand, and Becker jumped. 'Was that a story from your head, Grampa, or a real one?'

He scratched his chin. 'Mih stories is jest dat—stories.' He chuckled. Then he came back to Poplar Square. 'Traps always belong to the wise ones with sensitive ears. Don't you forget it, my boy!'

That's why I loved Grampa's stories. They were great when he told you them, but they were perfect when you found out what they *really* meant.

Chapter four

I hate magpies. Loads of them nest in the silver birches outside my window and I've decided they plan their early morning 'chacker, chacker, chacker' to bring me maximum suffering. I never get a lie-in because of them.

That Wednesday morning, I'm sure they were louder than ever. Grampa was snoring away. It was alright for him: he couldn't hear the magpies and he didn't have to get up for school either. I stretched, and felt my hand throb.

When I got up, the dressing on my finger was dull red. Mum soaked it off, and I winced as a streak of red spiralled through the salty water in the bowl.

'What's that face for?' she said, unwrapping another dressing. She was still mad at me. 'I've been doing some thinking.' She started to bind my hand up and I couldn't escape. 'So on Saturday,' she finished as she put the safety pin in, 'you'll come down to the Larches with me and apologise to Joe for lying.'

What I haven't told you yet is that my mum works for Leon Fuller. Yep, that's right: Joe's dad. She's worked at his old people's home for the last six years, and she's always sucking up to him. And that's why I have to be nice to Joe.

I left for school pretty early—one, to get away from Mum, and two, to be there on time. No way was I going to get a detention from 'Ansome on top of the two Mr Hogarth had given me. But my stomach was churning away. What would I say to Joe?

Inside the gate, the rugby crowd was hanging out.

'Over here, Morris.' Seb Phillips: big, loud and built like a wall. To be honest with you, I was scared of him, but it would be stupid to ignore him. I might be short-sighted, but I certainly wasn't deaf like Grampa—and I couldn't pretend I hadn't heard. I walked slowly across.

'Have you hurt your hand, Martin?' Andy Thompson: slighter, brighter and gentler, always noticing the details.

'It's nothing.' I put my hands in my pockets and found a stone to kick.

'Seen Facebook?' Shaun asked.

I shook my head and concentrated on the stone. I was desperate to find out what they were talking about, but I couldn't let on we didn't have a computer, could I?

'We worked it out about your rugby shirt yesterday, Morris. Fuller's a coward. So he's getting a pasting on Facebook, thanks to …' Seb put on a deep voice, like he was announcing a super-hero: 'Shaun Webster, the Wonder Webber!'

The others laughed, and I looked up for the first time. 'Thanks!' I muttered.

'Everyone's joining in,' said Andy. 'Loads of people have *Liked* it.'

'What did you do?' I asked. Why, oh why, did the bell have to go right then?

'We'd better go!' said Seb, slinging his bag over his shoulder. 'Why don't you come to the Plaza with us after school and we'll fill you in?'

The Plaza? With them? I went red. 'Can't. I'm in detention with Mr Hogarth.' It was a great excuse.

'Oh,' Seb nodded. He looked at Andy. 'Don't worry about that. We'll see if BB can work his magic.'

Andy smiled his big grin. He was always smiling. 'Glad you've got so much faith in me! I'll definitely give it a go.' They'd called Andy BB for a while, but I wasn't sure why. I shrugged. No way would Mr Hogarth change his mind.

Mr Anselm walked past on his way to the gate. 'Get to registration boys!' Then he saw me. 'Well, well! You're here, Michael.'

I said 'Martin, sir,' but he'd gone.

Shaun pulled a face behind his back. 'What a ...' But he stopped, and looked at Andy.

'Idiot?' Andy said. 'What an idiot!'

Seb laughed. 'OK, BB.' He turned to me. 'What we thought, Morris, is that you and Andy could swap places today. BB'll sit by Flabby and you can sit next to me.'

'Thanks.' I had thought the rugby lot couldn't care less, but perhaps I was wrong.

When we went to our form room, though, Joe wasn't there. Miss Lancelot read his name out and when she read it out again, Seb said 'Anorexia' under his breath. I laughed. I liked being in on the joke.

But it got even better than that. I was doing a boring worksheet in DT because I couldn't hold any tools, when Mr Hogarth came in. 'Martin, a little bird told me you didn't throw that shirt yesterday?'

'No, sir. I didn't even do PE. I'd been in the first aid room.'

'So who threw it then?'

I blushed. No way could I split on Joe.

'It was Fuller, wasn't it?' I nodded a tiny nod. Well, that wasn't telling, was it?

'And he's not in today, so I'll have to pick him up tomorrow. He'll be doing your detentions, Morris, so I won't be seeing you this afternoon.'

'Thanks, sir.'

Seb winked at me when he left.

'Who told him?' I asked.

He pointed at Andy with the piece of wood he was holding.

'Thanks, Andy,' I said, annoyed that I'd turned my usual shade of red.

'You're welcome.' He touched my arm. 'And it means you can come to the Plaza with us after all.' Before I could say any more, he pulled a fiver out of his pocket. 'It's OK. I'm paying.' Mr Wright spared my embarrassment by telling us to pack away.

I'd always walked home on my own, so after school, I did something for the very first time: I left with a couple of lads from my form. Mum wouldn't be expecting me for a while: after all, she thought I was in detention.

We could hear Bruno Tacchi belting out 'Halfway to Paradise' before we even opened the door to the Pizza Plaza. Bruno's a big Italian with greyish curly hair. He's always worked on Main Street but sounds like he only left Italy last week. 'So near, yet so far ...!' Bruno broke off singing. 'Gentlemen! Great to see you.' He left his stool at the counter and came across. 'Close the door quick. It's cold.' We smiled. Poor Bruno. It was always cold in England, according to him.

The Plaza wasn't your five star restaurant. The menus were covered in creased plastic and there was always sixties music playing, but I loved it. It was the only place teenagers were welcome. 'We love kids!' Bruno's wife Liza would say. And I didn't mind her calling me that.

We were the only ones in, so we grabbed the best table. It was behind a pillar and a fake lemon tree. It looked out onto the road and you could watch everyone going by and see everyone in the restaurant as well without being noticed yourself. Andy ordered the drinks and he and Seb filled me in on the Facebook thing. Shaun had found a picture of Joe, stuck his head on a Sumo wrestler's body and said what he'd done in PE.

'There were 84 *Likes* and loads of comments when I checked at lunchtime,' said Seb. 'Fuller's a thug. Why do you bother with him, Martin?'

I couldn't tell them, could I? So I changed the subject. 'I wonder where he was today?'

'Eating his way through a rubbish dump, I expect,' said Seb. I snorted, and bubbles fizzed up my nose.

Seb finished his drink and checked the pizza-faced clock over the counter. 'Better go. Trumpet lesson at half four.'

Chapter five

'**M**ore drinks, boys?' Bruno called over when Seb had gone.

Andy said 'Yes, please!' at the same time as I said 'No, it's fine.' I felt my ears go red. That always happens when I'm embarrassed. And you've guessed by now that's a pretty regular occurrence.

Bruno brought the drinks across and I racked my brains for something to say. Mum calls it small talk and I'm rubbish at it. The silence didn't seem to bother Andy, but I was nervous. And so I went and made a total fool of myself when I said in a rush, 'Why do they call you BB, when there isn't even a *B* in your name?'

Andy stirred his straw around in his drink and smiled. 'Bible Basher.' He paused. 'I'm a Christian, you see.' I went even redder. 'Not very cool, is it? But it's fine: they're only joking.' Andy cleared his throat. 'To be honest, I'm a bit ashamed of myself, Martin. I've never stuck up for you, and it's only cowards who don't speak up when they should. If you can put wrong things right, you should. I hate seeing the way you always take the rap for Joe. That's why I said something to Mr Hogarth.'

'Thanks,' I concentrated on drumming along on the table with my good hand to 'Stand By Me'. A Christian?

Surely they were pathetic and weak and ... well, not like
Andy?

'You didn't expect that, did you?' Andy said.

Before I could think of something to say, Bruno
came across. 'Heads down, lads.' He moved to the door.
'Good afternoon, sir. And you too. Come this way.' He
shepherded the new arrivals very firmly to a table on the
far side of the restaurant.

Andy and I froze. What on earth was Mr Anselm doing
in the Pizza Plaza? And much, much more to the point,
what on earth was Joe Fuller doing there with him? Bruno
played a blinder. He fussed around the pair of them before
coming across to our side of the restaurant. 'Don't move,'
he whispered. 'I'll make sure they don't know you're here.'

'Ansome had no volume control. He shouted, even
though he thought it was just him and Joe in the
restaurant.

'Here, Tacchi.' He was so rude: Bruno wasn't a dog! But
Bruno played it cool. He took his pencil from behind his
ear and a pad from his Italian flag apron pocket.

'And how are you keeping, Mr Anselm?'

'Fine. How's your Marco these days? Not in trouble like
he always was at school?' Joe sniggered.

Bruno didn't even look up. 'He's not long been promoted
to detective sergeant, Mr Anselm. He learnt so much when
he left you behind. Now, what can I get you?'

Andy made the 'perfect' sign and I smothered a laugh.

When Bruno walked away, the conversation changed.
'So they're bullying you on Facebook?'

'Yeah. I'll show you.' Peering through the fake lemon
tree, I could see Joe showing 'Ansome his phone.

'Don't worry,' said 'Ansome. 'I'll sort it.'

Bruno soon came out with a coffee for 'Ansome, a large Coke and a megabowl of profiteroles for Joe.

'All for me! All for me!' Joe was like a little kid. Andy pulled a face, but I was racking my brains. Where had I heard that before? Then I remembered: Grampa's story. Monkey. And the mangoes.

'Ansome sipped his coffee. 'So you've had a good day?' Joe nodded. 'You picked them up?'

Joe dug his fork into his bowl. 'Of course. No one suspected anything.'

'I've always said the only degree you ever need is from the university of life. And you're going the right way to get first class honours.'

Joe spoke with his mouth full. 'Thanks, Roy.'

Andy's jaw dropped. 'Roy?' he mouthed.

'Ansome was holding out his hand. 'Let's have them then.' Joe wiped his mouth on his sleeve and reached down. When he sat back up, he gave 'Ansome a bag with something orange in it. I wished for the millionth time I wasn't short-sighted. I couldn't for the life of me work out what it was.

'Fantastic! Chip off the old block, you are. So it's a green light for Saturday then—as long as you keep your mouth shut.'

Joe nodded. When he'd finished the profiteroles, 'Ansome settled the bill and they left.

Andy was straight on his phone. 'I'm texting Shaun to take the page down,' he said. 'We'll be for it tomorrow.'

'I don't get it, Andy,' I said. 'Did you see what Joe passed over?'

He sent the text and looked up. 'No idea.'

'Wow!' said Bruno. He pulled up a chair. 'There's a couple of nasties I don't like to see together. Both as bad as each other. There's something definitely not right there.' He took the red and white checked tea towel from his shoulder and pulled up a chair up. 'Boys, bad is ... bad. Andy, you know that from last week.'

Andy nodded. 'Tell Martin, Bruno.'

'I run 24-7, the youth group at Andy's church,' Bruno explained. 'Last week, we were discussing some of the horrible things that can happen and we can't do anything about. We discovered in the Bible that God never, ever, ever lets the baddies get away with it.' Bruno was getting "Italian excited", waving his hands around and speaking fast. 'No, no, no! He'll always make sure that justice will be done. You can find out some more from Andy or from 24-7 if you'd like to come?'

I didn't know what to say, so I fiddled with the bandage on my hand. Bruno stood up. 'I'll leave it with you. And let me know if you find out why those two fellas were in here together today.'

'Thanks, Bruno,' Andy said. 'We'll keep you posted.'

When we'd finished our drinks, we hung around at the corner for a couple of minutes.

'I'll fill Seb in,' Andy said. We high-fived with my good hand and went home with an awful lot to think about.

It wasn't too bad when I got in. Mum had worked a short shift, so she was in a good mood.

'That's one detention done,' she called.

I kicked my shoes off and went through to the kitchen. 'Good news. Mr Hogarth let me off.'

Mum narrowed her eyes. She always does that when she's suspicious. 'He believed it when the others told him about Joe ripping my shirt.'

She put the kettle on. 'So where've you been till now?'

'At the Plaza. With Andy. And Seb.'

She folded her arms. 'They're not your sort.'

'They've been great today, Mum.'

'Well, you're not ditching Joe.'

'But I don't still have to go and apologise to him on Saturday, do I?'

She was a bit flustered and picked up a glass instead of a mug. 'Too late. I've said you will, so ... that's that. Anyway, it'll do you no harm to be civil to the Fullers.'

The kettle started to boil. I said nothing. I knew there was absolutely no point.

Chapter six

I liked Thursdays. We had Art—my best subject. I made it in good time, and 'Ansome wasn't at the gate. Miss Lancelot smiled as I walked in. 'It's working, Martin. You're here on time again!'

'Thanks, Miss.'

'Four Eyes!' Joe was back, acting as if nothing had happened. I ignored him.

'Where's Andy and Seb?' I asked Miss Lancelot.

'Mr Anselm came for them. And Shaun.' Joe folded his arms and I caught his smirk. That was enough. 'Where are you going, Martin?'

'I forgot something, Miss,' I said as I headed for the door.

'Martin!' I heard her say, and I almost turned back, but I told myself, 'Go on! Go on!'

Seb and Shaun were outside 'Ansome's office in North Corridor. He was yelling at someone inside. 'What are you doing?' whispered Seb when he saw me. 'You're not in trouble.'

I ignored him. 'Andy?' I said, pointing at the door. They both nodded.

Shaun sounded panicky. 'Get out while you can.'

'No.' I couldn't believe how confident I sounded. 'I'm in on this too.'

'Get out!' The door shook on its hinges and Andy appeared, white-faced.

'In here, Webster!' 'Ansome's volume control had reached the danger zone, but when he saw me, he somehow went even louder. 'Michael! I didn't ask to see you.' Inside, I was all butterflies, but for some reason, my voice didn't wobble. And I don't think I went red either.

'Martin, sir, not Michael. And I need to speak to you.' 'Ansome was so shocked he couldn't think what to say. 'You see,' I continued in a rush, 'someone told me it's important to put wrong things right if you can.' I looked at Andy. 'It's only cowards who don't speak up. I hate seeing my friends get into trouble when it's someone else's fault.'

'Thanks,' Andy whispered.

'Ansome's right eyebrow twitched, and a strand of hair fell into his eyes. 'You think,' he started in a whisper, 'you think you know better than me?' He ended in a roar.

I pushed my glasses back up my nose. 'No sir, but ...'

'Ansome took full advantage. 'No sir, yes sir, three bags full sir!' He flicked the strand of hair away. 'Get to your form room now!'

'Go on Martin,' Andy murmured. There was a silence for what seemed like ages. Then the bell went for first lesson. I straightened up.

'I'm going, sir,' I said, then smiled. 'But I'll be back.' How come I'd remembered that? It was the most famous saying of my dad's all-time action film hero, Arnold Schwarzenegger. Somehow, it made me feel even better, and I walked off with a hint of Arnie in my stride.

About halfway through Art, Seb and Andy came in. They gave a note to Mr Bagshaw and went to the cupboard to get their work. Joe was on the front table working with chalk. When Seb and Andy came back, he wrote something on the table. They shook their heads and took their seats behind me in silence. Joe caught me staring and made glasses round his eyes with his fingers and thumbs. I went back to my drawing.

When Mr Bagshaw was helping one of the others, I took my yellow pencil to the bin to sharpen it. Seb and Andy didn't look up.

'Alright?' I whispered. 'Where's Shaun?'

'He's barracked with 'Ansome.'

Barracking was a nightmare. You had to sit in silence for a day in 'Ansome's office and work with your head down. Breathe in the wrong place, and you were on the skids.

'Martin,' Mr Bagshaw called.

'Just sharpening my pencil, sir.' I went back to my seat.

We were working from a photograph of Main Street. My sketch wasn't bad—even with a dodgy finger. I couldn't get the traffic lights in perspective, though, and took it up to Mr Bagshaw to see if he could help. As I walked past, even I could see Joe's was rubbish. He'd ruined the Pizza Plaza and the bank next door by putting stupid circles on them. On his desk was the rude sign he'd drawn when Seb and Andy went past.

Mr Bagshaw was pleased with my drawing. I smiled, leaned back and nudged Joe's desk. By accident. I think.

'Mind what you're doing,' Joe snapped. I stood aside and Mr Bagshaw looked up. There was no way he could miss Joe's additional 'artwork'.

'See me at the end of the lesson, Joe.'

37

'But sir,' Joe began. Mr Bagshaw, though, was having none of it. I shrugged and said sorry, but I didn't mean it. Of course I didn't. Joe was caught this time, and he couldn't wriggle his way out. I suddenly remembered Grampa's Anancy story again, and smiled to myself.

After Art, Andy and Seb filled me in on what had happened. They both had a detention for helping Shaun with the Facebook thing.

'You were amazing!' said Seb. 'I couldn't have turned up like you did.'

I felt proud—and more confident than I should have been. 'I'm going back at break.'

Andy gasped. 'Don't be stupid, Martin. What for? You're not even in trouble.'

'But I told 'Ansome I would. So I will.'

'Respect,' said Seb. No one had ever said that to me before, and I stood up straight. I could take 'Ansome on.

When Joe saw me, he gave me the eye. I guess he wanted me to feel scared, but I didn't. After the Pizza Plaza, I had something on him. For the first time ever, mine was the next move. And I would get him eventually. Once and for all.

I could hardly wait for the break bell, and when it went, I made my way to 'Ansome's office. He wasn't there, but Shaun was sat at a desk in the corner.

'Where's 'Ansome?'

'Gone for coffee. What are you doing here?' Shaun looked panicky. I wondered what had changed. Before, I would have been terrified—not him.

'I'll only be a minute,' I said, looking around the room. It was a long shot, but there might be something that would tell me why 'Ansome and Joe were together the day before. I peered at the walls. School rules, a bullying notice, fire procedures with Plowright eagles staring out from them. Nothing interesting. But there was somewhere else I could check. I stopped, took a deep breath, then went and sat in 'Ansome's chair.

Shaun gasped. 'What's got into you?' I grinned, and spun round once in the chair before setting to work. The desk was a mess: piles of papers and torn-off notes like confetti. I lifted them up and looked for anything that might give me a clue. Nothing.

Then I looked down. I put my hand on the desk drawer. No one would ever dare to do what I was about to do.

Shaun was scared stiff, out of his chair, almost dancing by the office door. 'Don't, Martin, please don't!'

I opened the drawer.

'He's coming!' Shaun shot back to his seat, and I slid underneath the desk.

The door opened. 'You behaving?' 'Ansome grunted.

'Yes, sir,' Shaun said. Then he played a blinder. 'I need the toilet sir.'

'Ansome huffed. The desk above me clunked. His coffee mug. I ducked, my heart thudding so loudly I was sure he'd hear it. 'I didn't go into teaching to take stupid boys to the toilet. But I suppose this is what we've come to.' Shaun's chair scraped back. The door slammed and they were gone.

I breathed hard and came out from under the desk. At the most, I had a few minutes. I went back to the drawer, rifled through and claimed my prize. Mission accomplished.

I closed the drawer and strolled out, my hands firmly in my pockets. James Bond had nothing on me.

Chapter seven

Andy was pacing up and down at the top of North Corridor. 'What happened?'

'Guess.'

'You didn't get caught, did you?'

'Nope. I got out alive. And ...' I decided I quite liked dramatic pauses. 'I've brought these with me.'

I slowly pulled out what I'd pocketed from 'Ansome's drawer. An envelope with 'Golden Larches' stamped on it, addressed to Mr R Anselm. And a wristband. I thought Andy's eyes would pop out of his head. A fluorescent orange wristband.

It was a long day. Seb and Andy were doing their detention at lunch and I was worried about meeting Joe, so I went to Art. Mr Bagshaw gave me two reward points for going in for extra work, but I didn't spend much time drawing. I took the letter from the Golden Larches envelope and unfolded it. The handwriting was a scrawl—worse than mine—and I had to take my glasses off to make it out:

Roy

Hardware ready. Joe on pick-up on 16th. Test run on 17th.

Bravo November Romeo 58 Oscar Lima Echo.

If all OK, we're on for 19th.

Leon.

Apart from letting me know the obvious—that there was definitely a link between the Fullers and 'Ansome—it made no sense to me at all.

*   *   *

'Have you read it?' Big Seb asked as we left at the end of the day. He was desperate to see the letter. 'C'mon, Action Man!'

Before I could take the envelope out of my rucksack, I was jabbed in the ribs. Joe. He got in front of us and turned around. 'Mummy's boy's coming to see me on Saturday!'

'Don't push it, Joe,' Andy said calmly.

Joe carried on walking backwards. 'Why? What'll you do about it?'

A cleaner a few metres away had put her mop and bucket down to lock the cupboard. Let's just say that the next few seconds was like one of those old black and white films where the fat man always ends up in trouble and you laugh because you can see it coming. Joe tripped over the bucket, fell and his backside got wedged in it. He was furious.

'You stupid …' He turned on the cleaner, who was laughing too.

'Way to go, Fuller,' Seb said, as we walked past.

Andy stopped. 'Wait a minute.' He went back and held out his hand, but Joe was having none of it.

'Get lost, you …' and swore before he said 'Bible Basher'. He pushed Andy away as he scrambled to get up. 'It'll be BB alright. And sooner than you think!'

We all stared at each other. Joe had well and truly lost the plot. He started to make his way to the door when a familiar voice shouted, 'Fuller! Where d'you think you're going?' Mr Hogarth. 'You're in detention, remember?'

Joe came back with a face like thunder. He barged me as he went past. 'You've got it coming to you—all of you!' he shouted back over his shoulder.

'I wonder what he's going on about?' Andy said. 'Still, it was worth a try. Love your enemies and all that.'

'Oh forget him,' Seb said. 'Let's go to the park and get our heads round that letter.'

I wondered whether to lie or not, but I caught Andy's eye. 'Can't,' I said. 'I have to look after my Grampa.'

Seb wasn't for giving up. 'Shall we come to your place then?'

I went a lovely shade of pink. Annoying. James Bond never did that—or Arnie Schwarzenegger for that matter. Seb and Andy lived on the posh estate. Sure, they'd been nice to me, but if they saw where we lived? I couldn't risk it.

Andy came to my rescue. 'How about the park at half seven tonight? Could you make that, Martin?'

'Probably,' I nodded. 'For half an hour or so.'

Seb had loads of homework to catch up on, so he couldn't. 'You go ahead,' he said, 'else we'll be wasting time. Let's have a quick look now, though.' I unfolded the letter and we all stared at it. But it was no use. None of us could figure it out.

* * *

We had tea, and Grampa settled down to watch his favourite soap.

'I'm taking Becker out, Grampa,' I called from the hallway. 'I'll be back in half an hour. Now, mind my hand, Becker!' I said as he strained for the door.

It was quietish on Main Street. I waved to Bruno in the Plaza, but he was busy. Becker was eyeing a cat across the road. 'This way,' I said, but he was all for going in the opposite direction. Because of him, I bumped into a man standing outside the bank. 'Sorry.'

'Watch where you're going!' I half took in the man. He was really big, but his lips were thin, so thin, it was like they weren't there. Becker started to sniff around him. He can be a real pain like that sometimes.

'Sorry,' I said again. 'He's only being friendly. Come on, Becker.' For some stupid reason, he wouldn't budge. He kept doing that low growl thing in his throat and jumping up. The man was getting annoyed. And so was I. I pulled and pulled, but Becker was having none of it.

'Get him off me!' the man shouted. And then he did something terrible: he lashed out with his boot. Becker yelped and fell back.

'Hey, you can't do that! I looked into the man's face properly for the first time. His wafer thin lip curled. Becker was whining, and I shook as I kneeled down on the pavement to him. The man went to kick again and I ducked. What would have happened next if his phone hadn't gone off, goodness knows. He snarled as he answered it. 'Roy. That you?'

I froze. The caller's volume was unmistakable: 'Ansome! I had to stay and listen. The man was nervous with me around, but I was going nowhere. I focused on Becker so he wouldn't suspect me, but all the time I was straining to catch what he was saying.

'Five minutes? OK. I'll text as soon as I see it.'

Becker was up, but the park was out of the question. He was limping, and we crawled along Main Street. When almost four minutes were gone, I glanced back. The man seemed to have forgotten about us and was watching the road. I sat down on a window ledge and put Becker on my left. That way, I could look too. I waited. A few cars came past: an Astra, a red Fiat Bravo, a Focus. Nothing unusual. They stopped for the lights. If the driver of the Bravo hadn't revved a bit, I wouldn't have looked again. 'Ole!' I said out loud. 'Ole! O-L-E!' I like Spanish, but that wasn't why. O, L and E were the last three letters on the number plate.

I jumped up and Becker yelped. 'Sorry Becks.' I sat back down and took the letter from my pocket: *Bravo November Romeo 58 Oscar Lima Echo.* 'Becker, I've got it! It's the reg of that red Bravo!' I looked back to the traffic lights. The man with no lips had gone.

It was twenty past seven. I texted Andy. 'I'm not going to make it.' Then I took a deep breath and went for it. 'Come round to mine if you like. 4c Poplar Square.' And I headed home.

I carried a whimpering Becker up the stairs and he flopped at Grampa's feet. When I told him what happened—or some of it—he said, 'He's like you with your finger, Martin. Get me a bag of peas and a tea-towel.' Grampa wrapped the frozen peas around Becker's leg, put him on the settee and made a fuss of him.

Chapter eight

When the doorbell went, Grampa was surprised. 'Your mother's not home already?'

He was even more surprised when Andy came in and shook his hand. No one from school had ever visited before.

Grampa told Andy what had happened to Becker, and I couldn't wait to tell him the rest. I was going to suggest we went to my room, but I was worried what he'd think of me sharing with my Grampa, so we stayed in the living room. It wasn't long before Grampa started to doze, and I filled Andy in.

'So let's get this straight,' Andy said. He concentrated hard, pausing after each sentence. 'Something's going to happen on Saturday. Joe's involved. And his dad. And 'Ansome too.' I nodded. 'And now there's the man at the bank.'

'And the Bravo driver,' I said.

'Yes, unless the driver was Joe's dad—or 'Ansome.'

I hadn't thought of that. 'But what exactly was that man timing?'

'If we knew that,' said Andy, 'we'd probably be able to work the rest of it out, wouldn't we?'

My mouth had gone all dry and I felt a bit hot. 'I don't get it, Andy. And I don't like it either. Something dodgy's going on.'

'Shame it's not 24-7 until Monday,' Andy said.

'24-7?'

'Youth club,' Andy reminded me.

'Why?'

'Because, like Bruno said, at the moment we're finding out about bad people and how they never win in the end. That's because God's in control, even when things like this are way out of ours. I was thinking that perhaps one of the leaders at 24-7 might have some ideas about what we could do.'

I was curious. 'Why 24-7?'

'The name?' I nodded. 'Well, it reminds us of a couple of things. First, if we're Christians, we never stop being one. And second, to help others to find out what's great about God any time they ask—day or night! But 24-7's our motto as well, a bit like at school.'

'Be strong; reach high!' we both said at once, like we had to in assembly when the Plowright eagles came up on the screen. When we stopped laughing, Andy carried on.

'24-7 is loads better than that though. It's from the Bible. I don't know if you know, but the Bible's divided into books, and chapters, and then little sections called verses.' I shook my head. 'In one of the older books called Exodus, a great leader named Moses passed on God's instructions to help his people to live great lives. In chapter 24 and verse 7, after they'd heard what he had to say, the people said, "We will do everything the Lord has said." When we were looking for a motto, we thought that was great. What could be better than doing what God wants for your life? So that's why it's 24-7.'

Andy knew so much about the Bible and it seemed he believed it. I didn't get that. I'd never met anyone like him before. But whatever he was, he wasn't a Bible Basher. He was really gentle. And kind.

Becker twitched in his sleep and Andy's phone buzzed. He checked it and stood up. 'That's my mum after me. I'll have to go,' he said. 'Let's fill Seb in tomorrow and see if we can work anything else out. Come to mine for tea if you like.'

'I'll ask,' I said.

Grampa woke up when Andy had gone. 'Lovely young man! Much nicer than the Fuller boy.'

When we finally went to bed, the evening was like a film on constant rewind in my head: the man outside the bank; Becker; 24-7. And as much as I tried to distract myself, I couldn't get the cars right. All I could hear was Bravos up and down Main Street.

Friday was wet. Very wet. But I didn't care. Mum had said I could go to Andy's for tea. I think she was feeling guilty about making me go to the Fullers, but she'd never admit that.

'Ansome was on the gate as usual at school, his black umbrella dripping. I wanted to get in the dry, but he stopped me.

'Here on time *again*, Michael? In that case, you can do a little job for me.' I'm sure he tilted his brolly on purpose. 'Sorry Michael. You got wet there.' I didn't say anything, not even to correct my name. Let him think I was stupid. Like Anancy. And Monkey.

'Joe Fuller's in your form, isn't he?' As if he didn't know! I said nothing, just waited. 'Ansome was getting fed up. 'Tell him to come and see me at break—if there's a tongue in your head.'

The last thing I wanted to do was talk to Joe, but something I wanted to do less was spend time with 'Ansome. 'Yes, sir,' I muttered.

'Hey!' he shouted after me.

'Sorry, sir.' I couldn't possibly have guessed that he'd get soaked if I stamped in the next puddle, could I?

Andy was already sitting next to Joe in our form room.

'Message from 'Ansome,' I said. Joe looked up. 'He wants to see you at break.'

In Geography, Mr Carter was in a good mood, and particularly when I volunteered to take a stack of books to the staffroom in North Corridor at the end of the lesson. When I'd done it, I waited in the shadow of a cupboard until I saw Joe bundling along, looking for all the world like an overfed insect. He disappeared into 'Ansome's office.

I tiptoed down the corridor after him and leaned against the wall. My palms were sweaty, but I shot a quick look through the glass panel in the door. Joe was sitting on the edge of 'Ansome's desk with his back to me, and 'Ansome was in his chair, his hands behind head. I leaned in and listened hard.

'You're absolutely sure about Morris? I don't trust that boy.'

I rocked on my heels and only just managed to stop myself from grabbing the door handle to keep my balance.

'Four Eyes? Believe me, Roy, he'll be fine. He owes me big time and he's too wet to say no. In any case, his mother'll make him do it if my dad says so.'

'You're certain? It'll all depend on him, you know.'

'Trust me. You know how dumb he is—as well as half-blind! He'd never mess with me.'

That was enough. I made my way to Spanish. Señor Huerta picked me up twice for not concentrating, and I was lucky not to get a detention. When lunchtime came, the others could hardly believe what I told them.

'Wow! What on earth did he mean?'

'I don't know, but it doesn't sound good, does it?' I felt a bit sick.

'We're going away this weekend,' said Seb. 'Sorry about that. I really want to be here for you.'

Andy could see the way I was feeling. 'Don't worry, Martin. I'm not going anywhere. We'll sort it.'

The day dragged by. When the bell went for the end of school, I'd never been so pleased.

Joe caught me off guard, pulling my rucksack straps, and I stumbled backwards. I felt his breath on the back of my neck once more. 'My place. Tomorrow. Ten o'clock. Don't forget, Four Eyes.'

Chapter nine

Andy's mum was cooking when we went in.
'So you're Martin?' she said. 'Great to meet you.
I'd shake your hand, but ...' We both laughed. Whatever
was in the mixing bowl was all over her fingers too.

'That's OK.' I'm rubbish at meeting new people, but she
didn't seem to notice.

'Take Martin through to the dining room, Andy,' she
said. 'I've left you some bits and pieces on the table.' I
went to take my shoes off and she laughed again. 'Don't
bother, Martin. No one else does in this house!'

The Thompsons' dining room was what my mum would
call a 'domestic disaster'. She hated mess. Besides the
table and the sideboard, there was a piano with loads of
stuff piled on the top, books and magazines on the piano
stool, a mountain of ironing in a basket and a lopsided
stack of folders which looked as though it would topple
any minute. Perhaps they weren't as posh as I thought?

Andy saw me looking around. 'It's always like this in
here!' he said, and I blushed. We grabbed a can each and
some chocolate. Andy smiled. 'You must be special. We
normally only get plain biscuits and squash.' He wandered
over to the piano, hit a couple of notes, then rifled through
the stuff on the top. Eventually, he slipped out a piece of

paper with a house drawn on it. He turned it over and it was blank on the other side.

'Emma's,' he said. 'She won't mind.' Emma was Andy's little sister.

Next, he went over to the windowsill and found a pen in a pot. After scribbling with it for a couple of seconds, it came to life.

We sat down at the table, and Andy wrote 'The Facts' at the top of the page. 'Now where's the letter?' he said.

I pulled it out of my bag, and we wrote down what we knew.

1. *Something's happening on Saturday.*

2. *There's a red Fiat Bravo: NR58 OLE.*

3. *People: ROY* (we laughed)*, Joe, Joe's dad, the man outside the bank, Bravo driver???*

4. *Joe did a pick-up on Wednesday when he wasn't at school.*

5. *Hardware.*

6. *Orange wristbands.*

7. *Martin???*

Andy sucked the pen. Then he drew a line and wrote 'What we don't know'. In massive letters, he wrote 'WHY?' We stared and stared, as if the paper was going to help us. Nothing.

Andy doodled down the margin. 'It doesn't make any sense, does it?'

'Nope.'

'But,' said Andy, 'it will tomorrow, and that's for certain.' He rapped the pen on the table. 'I'm worried, Martin.'

I swallowed. 'Me too.'

'So what do we do? Tell our parents?'

I traced the diamond pattern on the tablecloth with my good hand. 'No way. My Grampa always says my imagination works overtime. Who'd believe me?'

'We were talking about this last night, weren't we?' said Andy. 'Bad stuff and bad people. God's dealt with it, but ...'

'How?' The question was out. I'd thought and thought about what Andy had said about God being in control, and I wanted to know more.

'How?' Andy sucked his pen for a moment, then drew a star on the paper. 'Martin, do you remember the Christmas story? Mary, Joseph, the shepherds and all that?'

'Yeah. I was the innkeeper in our nativity play in Year 3.'

Andy laughed. 'Better than me. I was a sheep!' Then he looked serious again. 'It's not just a story for kids at Christmas, though. You see, the baby Jesus was God's Son who chose to be born and to live and to die.'

That was news to me. 'Go on,' I said.

'We have to make choices all the time—though not like the choice Jesus made to come to earth. And most people choose to live as if God isn't there. But he is,' Andy continued, 'and he knows about all our dumb choices as well as the good ones. Trust me, there's plenty I've made that I wouldn't want anyone to know about, let alone God, who's perfect. And the bad things we've chosen to do, they should be dealt with. That's only fair, isn't it?'

I nodded. It sounded pretty logical. How many things had I kept quiet because I was scared of what'd happen if my mum found out?

Andy carried on, 'And that's why Jesus was born. He became a human like us, except he was perfect. He chose to help people and showed them what God was really like. But in the end they killed him. Am I making any sense?' Andy asked. I nodded, even though I was a bit confused. It didn't sound very fair to me.

He carried on. 'All the time, though, God was in control. He knew what would happen as it was part of his great plan. When Jesus died, he took the rap for every bad choice we've ever made. He didn't have to, but he was willing to swap places with us so we wouldn't need to face God's punishment.' Andy dried up and put the lid on his pen. He'd gone a bit red, and I knew what that felt like, so I took my glasses off and cleaned them on my shirt to give him a break.

'Set the table for me, Andy,' his mum called.

Andy went to the sideboard for some knives and forks. 'If you want to know any more,' he said, 'just let me know.'

Deep down, I did. How many bad choices had I made? I couldn't begin to count. But the answer to all that was Jesus? I hadn't thought of him outside RE before. And certainly not about him and me.

'I was just thinking,' Andy came across with the cutlery, 'we should have a secret signal in case things go wrong tomorrow.'

'That's a great idea. They did that in a film I saw.' I racked my brains, then shook my head. 'I can't think of one, though.'

'Me neither,' said Andy. 'But we will.'

Dinner was good. It didn't take long to demolish the shepherd's pie, and then Andy's mum came in with the pudding.

She smiled. 'Would you like some Pink, Martin?'

I stared. 'Pink?'

'When Emma was little,' Andy's mum explained, 'she couldn't say "strawberry mousse", so she called it Pink. And the name stuck.'

'Pink,' said Andy, thoughtfully. He looked at me. 'Pink!'

'What?'

'Signal,' he whispered. 'No one will get it!'

I laughed. 'Superb!'

'What are you talking about?' Emma asked.

'Don't whisper at the table, Andy,' his mum said, before turning to me. 'Do you have anything planned for the weekend, Martin?'

My stomach tightened. 'Not really. Only going to where my mum works in the morning and looking after my Grampa after that.'

Chapter ten

Saturday morning wasn't pleasant. I'll admit I can be grumpy when I want to, and that morning, I was at my 'best worst', if you know what I mean. I dragged my feet getting ready. Mum had to be at work at ten, so she was pretty stressed when I was still cleaning my teeth with only twenty minutes to go.

We reached the Golden Larches at ten o'clock on the dot. 'See. Told you we'd make it,' I said. Mum just huffed. She pressed the code to get in, but the door opened before she could turn the handle. Leon Fuller stood there in his leather jacket and designer jeans.

He tapped his watch. 'Ten o'clock pre-cise-ly.'

'Sorry, Mr Fuller. I'm so sorry. Problems at home.' My mum's pretty strong, as you know, but she turns into a gibbering wreck when Fuller's around. 'Martin's here, Mr Fuller.'

'Yes,' he said. 'I *can* see.' Mum hesitated for a moment and Fuller clapped his hands. 'Off you go, Leticia. Remember I pay you to work, not to stand around all day.'

My mother scuttled off. 'Sorry, Mr Fuller.'

'You,' he said when she'd gone. 'Come with me.'

There was a little room at the back of the Larches which was used as a store. You could find just about anything in there: sheets, tablecloths, boxes, scooters, wheelchairs, zimmer frames, even an old mattress or two. When I was little and Mum was on a late shift, I used to play in there for ages with Joe—games he always won. That was where Fuller took me.

He opened the door and it smelt like towels when they're put away damp. I coughed. In front of the window, Joe was standing with his arms crossed, blocking out the sunshine. When Fuller flicked the light on, a cobweb trailing from the fake chandelier was illuminated and I remembered Anancy again. My heart beat fast. This time, I was Monkey: stuck, with no way of escape.

'Sit down.' Leon Fuller pressed a bit too hard on my shoulder. A bench was piled with blankets and pillows and I perched on the end. I tried not to look scared, but I was.

'So. My Joe's had two detentions because of you.' I said nothing. Fuller waited a moment before he slid down next to me. I tried to make room for him, but I couldn't. Without any warning, he twisted my ear. I winced. 'That isn't playing by the rules.' He twisted my ear harder. 'Is it, Morris?'

'No.' The word squeaked out of me and Joe laughed. His father winked at him and joined in. What was spooky was he laughed just like 'Ansome.

'Not so clever without BB and the others, are you, Four Eyes?' Joe sneered. And he was right. I was the old Martin again.

'BB, BB, BB!' his father laughed the 'Ansome laugh again, a gold filling flashing in his mouth. 'Now there's a thing!' Then as quickly as he started, he stopped. 'So, I have a couple of choices. I could—unfortunately—find out that your mother has done something wrong. It's a pity:

she's a good worker, Leticia, but there's plenty more where she came from.'

'Ooh Dad, that would be good,' said Joe. 'They might even get thrown out of their *lovely* flat.'

Leon Fuller twisted my ear another time and my glasses almost fell off. 'Or ...' he pushed them roughly back up my nose. 'I could give you a little job I need doing tonight, and then we'd call it quits.'

My ear was so sore, it was almost beyond pain. 'So,' he whispered, his face in mine, 'what's it to be?'

My eyes watered. 'Leave my mum out of this. Tell me what you want me to do.'

When I left the Golden Larches, I had my orders—and a throbbing ear. I texted Andy.

In the park, we sat on the swings. 'That man's a brute,' he said. 'You should go to the police.'

'My word against his and Joe the only witness?' I touched my glowing earlobe. 'At least we chose the right code word.'

Andy's mouth twitched. 'Yeah—that's pink alright.' Then he was serious again. 'Martin, you must tell someone.'

'When my mum's job is on the line?' I twisted the chains on the swing and faced Andy. 'He's got me every which way, hasn't he? So now let me tell you what he wants me to do.'

Andy was lost for words when I told him. 'Let me get this straight. He ... he wants you to sit in the Plaza? The Plaza? At seven o'clock?' I nodded. 'But that's mad. What for?'

'Don't ask me,' I said. 'But I'm sure it's not for a pizza.'

'And how long do you have to stay there for?'

I spun round and untwisted the chains. 'Dunno. He said it would be obvious when I should leave.' I fished in my pocket. 'Oh, and one more thing. I have to wear this.'

Andy gasped: a fluorescent orange wristband, exactly the same as the one I took from 'Ansome's desk. He shook his head. 'I don't like this one little bit.' We sat in silence, only the swings creaking. Then Andy coughed. 'Martin?'

'Yep?'

'I pray about things when I'm stuck. What d'you reckon?'

What was I meant to say? 'Whatever.'

'Thanks,' said Andy. I glanced sideways to see if he'd kneel down or put his hands together, but he just sat there and started talking. 'Father God, you already know what's going to happen. Please show us what to do, and please protect Martin from wrong things and bad people.'

My face was as red as my ear as I muttered something which sounded like 'Amen'. Wasn't that what you were supposed to do?

The swing creaked as Andy jumped off. 'Come on,' he said. 'Let's go and see Bruno.' That was the best move of the day. 'But before we do ...' Andy rolled back his sleeve. 'I can beat Mr Fuller any day.' On his arm were two fluorescent yellow wristbands. 'Here.' He looked at them quickly and took one off. 'You have this one.'

I couldn't see the difference until Andy pointed it out. Mine said 'PUSH' and his said 'FROG'. 'Yours means *Pray Until Something Happens*,' he explained, 'and mine's *Fully Rely On God*.' He went quiet for a moment. 'I don't have any bright ideas, Martin, but if you let Jesus into your life, he'll be in control. That's the best choice you could ever make. I've done that, so I know I can fully rely on God to look after me right now.'

I twisted the band around in my hand for a moment or two, running my fingers over the letters. Then I put it on.

Andy gave me the thumbs-up. 'That's it! Now, let's go.'

Saturday lunchtimes were always busy at the Plaza. 'We're full, boys!' Bruno shouted across as he expertly balanced four plates of pizza up his arm.

'We'll wait,' Andy said. We made our way to the counter and sat on the stools. There were families and shoppers in and a children's party at the far end of the restaurant. Bruno's favourite, 'It's Now or Never', was playing. We knew the words, as it was on so often. Bruno said it had something to do with Italy, but we didn't believe him. He was singing at the top of his voice as he came out with a birthday cake. Once the candles were blown out, he came across. 'Great to see you, lads. I'll get you a menu.'

'No thanks,' Andy said.

Bruno raised an eyebrow. 'Not eating in my restaurant? Now that *is* serious.'

'Do you have any bookings for tonight, Bruno? At 7ish?'

'I'm sure we must.' Bruno opened the big brown diary. 'Let's see. Oh yes: a table for one.' He looked up. 'Well, there's a thing. You'll never guess who it's for.' Bruno took the pencil from behind his ear. 'It's for Leon Fuller. And he's asked for the table by the window. So do you want me to book you one? Or would you prefer it later when Mr F has gone?'

Andy stopped him. 'Bruno, you remember you said to come back if we found out any more about the Mr Anselm thing?

'Yes?'

'Well, we have. And we think it's linked to Fuller's table tonight.' Andy was cut short by Liza calling for Bruno. He rolled his eyes. 'Let me get a couple of dinners out and it should quieten down.'

Twenty minutes later, we'd told Bruno the whole story.

Chapter eleven

'So let me get this straight,' Bruno was frowning hard. 'You think something's planned for this evening, Mr Fuller and Mr Anselm are involved and you're part of it now too?'

'Yep,' I said. 'That's pretty much it. But we can't work out any more than that.'

Bruno scratched his head. 'Me neither. But leave it with me. I'll see if I can think of anything. You turn up as planned and I'll be here for you.' He stopped. Then his dark eyes lit up. 'Hey! Shouldn't we have a signal of some sort in case anything happens?'

'Something pink!' we chorused, and laughed.

Bruno shook his head. 'Something pink? I don't get it!'

'It doesn't matter,' Andy said. 'But get hold of something pink for a signal.'

When we left, I felt better because Bruno knew, even though he didn't have any answers.

'You're not on your own tonight, Martin,' Andy said. 'Bruno'll be inside, and I'm going to be out here the whole time with Emma's pink socks!'

I shook my head. 'You mustn't, Andy. You've been great, but I don't want you getting caught up in anything nasty.'

'I've said I'll be here,' Andy said quietly, 'and God will be with me too: he'll take care of me.' There was a lump in my throat and I didn't know what to say. 'FROG!' said Andy. I was puzzled until he held out his wrist.

'Got it! PUSH,' I replied.

Andy touched my arm. 'See you later.'

'Thanks. I mean it.' He nodded, and we went our separate ways.

* * *

At twenty to seven, Mum was almost pushing me out of the door. 'Go on,' she said, 'you mustn't be late.' Fuller had spun her some yarn about the job I was doing and she'd fallen for it, of course.

I took my jacket off the peg, picked up Becker's lead and whistled. He came through, his tail wagging.

Mum's eyes narrowed. 'And where's he going?'

My hands shook as I knelt down and put the lead on. 'He hasn't had a walk today.'

'But Mr Fuller didn't say anything about the dog. I don't think he should go. You mustn't upset Mr Fuller.'

Becker's limp was almost gone and he was yapping, excited to go out. I stood up. 'He didn't say I couldn't take him, so he's coming with me.'

'Martin, come back!' But I didn't. Becker and I raced down the steps and her voice faded.

My heart pounded as I walked towards Bruno's place, but up and down Main Street everything was exactly as it should be. The Plaza sign swung in the breeze and the striped awning rattled. I checked my watch: ten to seven.

Somewhere, a magpie squawked and I jumped. Stupid bird. I clipped Becker's lead to the railings. 'Wait there,' I patted him. 'And bark the loudest you can if anything strange happens.' Becker wagged his tail and lay down.

I pushed open the Plaza door and listened. Early evening on a Saturday was very different from lunchtime. It was too late for families and too soon for adults. There was only one other table occupied. Some guys were eating pizzas and chatting. Nothing too suspicious there.

'Evening, Martin.' Bruno looked serious. 'You OK?'

'The Sun Ain't Gonna Shine Anymore' was playing. I tried to make a joke of it. 'Is that song for me?'

Bruno half smiled. 'Don't be daft. Now, you know where you're sitting.'

I went to the window seat and Bruno came across and peered out. 'I haven't seen anything out of the ordinary.' He shot a glance at the other table. 'They're OK,' he whispered. 'I checked them out earlier. Now, I'll get you a Coke. It's the least I can do. And remember ...' He pulled a bright pink serviette out of his apron pocket and left it on the table.

Bruno's salt and pepper pots were little towers of Pisa. I picked up a leaning cellar, poured some salt out and made a crossroads, but it was wobbly because my finger shook.

I almost jumped out of my skin when Bruno brought my drink across. As I put my hand to the straw, I saw the flash of orange under my sleeve. So I put my arm down, took the other wristband off and ran it through my fingers. 'PUSH,' I thought. 'PUSH.' I looked at the salty cross I'd made on the table, and everything Andy had told me about

Jesus came flooding back. And I did something I've never done before. I think it was praying, even if it was in my head. 'If you can hear me, God, I'm sorry for all the stupid choices I've made. I can't get my head around it, but thank you that Jesus was prepared to face you and take the punishment I deserved.'

It was right then that Becker started barking. He was up on his feet, straining at something across the road.

'Bloomin' dog,' I heard one of the men on the other table say. He stood up and stared out of the window.

In the moment he'd distracted me, I'd missed something outside. Standing directly across the road from me was the man with no lips. My heart was pounding, and I pushed my sleeve back, the orange band almost luminous on my wrist. Becker was still barking as the man raised something level with his eye. I saw a flash of orange and panicked. I reached for the pink serviette.

A man on the other table jumped up, and the next few moments seemed to go in slow motion. There was a crack, and the window shattered into a giant spider's web. I was knocked off my chair, and I must have hit my head as I went down.

When I came round, I shook my head and tried to sit up.

'No, no, no! Stay still, Martin!' Liza's voice seemed a long way away.

I was confused. 'I've cut my finger.' My voice sounded like it was inside a tunnel, echoey and strange.

'Your finger? If only …'

I opened my eyes a fraction and my head throbbed. The blurry edge of the table cloth was above my head.

'I need my glasses,' I said and reached out, but Liza put her hand on my shoulder.

'Don't move, Martin. You mustn't, you really mustn't!'

There were gravelly bits under my fingers and I felt so sleepy, I wondered if I was dreaming.

Liza kept talking. 'Don't go to sleep, Martin! Stay with me!'

'Martin!' Another voice broke in.

My throat was dry, but I croaked out, 'Andy?' He and Liza seemed a long way away. Just as they were disappearing, I saw two discs of light in front of me and for some reason I remembered our Art lesson. I choked out the word 'Circles.'

'Shhh,' Liza said, stroking my hair, which was a bit embarrassing.

'What did you say, Martin?' Andy sounded desperate.

'Circles. Joe's picture. The bank.'

And that was it. I was gone.

Chapter twelve

When I woke up again, I was in hospital. My eyelids felt like something was weighing them down. I turned my head to one side, squinted, then closed my eyes again.

'He's waking up!' It was my mum.

A machine was bleeping and a man's voice said, 'Martin, can you hear me?'

I tried to say yes, but I couldn't, and heard myself moan instead. I opened my left eye a fraction and the man was leaning right over me with a pen. Pinpricks of white burned into my eyes—too bright.

It was another couple of hours before I properly woke up, and I was in a different place. Mum was still there and her eyes went all shiny when I said hello. I had something stuck in my arm rigged up to a bag on a stand, and there were lots of machines. My head felt heavy, and Mum said I mustn't touch it. I didn't want to anyway.

Before she went, I asked her if the window was mended in the Pizza Plaza. That made her happy for some reason, and she told the next person who came in, 'He's remembered something!' Then she said, 'We'll talk about all that tomorrow, Martin.'

Tomorrow came soon enough. I discovered a bandage on my head, and I'd begun to remember some more, but I couldn't be sure if it was right. It felt weird—and scary too.

I was stuck in a room on my own. Lots of hospital people came in and out, but every time I asked what had happened, no one seemed to want to talk. Charlie was looking after me. 'Don't you worry about what happened, Martin,' he said, checking the bag on the stand. 'You just concentrate on getting well.'

Why do people say stupid things like that?

When my mum came in, she said, 'You look a bit better this morning. You don't know how lucky you are, Martin. Me too: lucky you're still here.' And she kissed me. I pulled a face, and she changed the subject. 'How are you feeling?'

'My head's killing.' I took a deep breath. 'Mum? Did what I think happened really happen?'

She fussed over the bedclothes. 'What do you reckon?'

'Someone took a shot at me, didn't they?'

She changed the subject. 'Before you say any more, some people would like to see you. Charlie says you're probably well enough, but only if you feel up to it.'

'Who is it?'

'The police. They want to talk to you.'

So it wasn't a bad dream after all. I shivered and slid further down the bed.

Mum went out and came back with two men in jeans and hoodies. They didn't look much like policemen to me. Charlie poked his head around the door. 'Only ten minutes, gentlemen.' They nodded. He closed the door and left us to it.

'Hi Martin, I'm Phil.'

'And I'm Marco,' the dark-haired one said. 'Marco Tacchi.'

But I wasn't listening. I stared at them both very carefully. Why were they so familiar?

They exchanged glances, and the dark-haired one tried again. 'I'm Bruno's son. Bruno? At the Pizza Plaza?'

'The Plaza. You were there ...'

Marco nodded. 'Your memory's working? That's great! Yes, we were on the other table last night. Sorry my dad couldn't let on, but we were working undercover, you see.'

My head ached as I concentrated, but I tried to ignore it. 'And one of you attacked me.'

'Not exactly,' said Phil. 'But let's take it a bit at a time. You go back as far as you can, and then we'll fill you in. Deal?' I nodded and he took out his notebook. 'So how exactly did all this begin?'

Slowly, I began to tell them the story: the rugby shirt, Joe and 'Ansome at the Plaza, the letter, the wristbands and the red Bravo. I told them about the man on Main Street and the deal with Fuller. Mum got upset then. 'Oh, Martin, if only I'd believed you.'

Phil asked me lots of questions until we ended up at the Plaza again. 'The last thing I remember is someone knocking me to the floor.' My hand went to the bandage on my head, and Mum gently took it away.

'That was me, Martin,' Phil said. 'I think it's fair to say you might not ... be here if I hadn't done that. You see, someone did take a shot at you from across the road. If I hadn't knocked you off your chair, you would have ended up on the wrong end of a BB gun. So I did you a favour, even if it doesn't feel like it at the moment.'

'BB gun?' I opened my eyes. It suddenly made sense. BB wasn't Andy at all! For the Fullers, those letters were a sick joke. And that's what Joe must've meant when he told us we had it coming to us.

'Thank goodness your dog gave the alarm,' Phil said.

'Becker! Is he OK?'

'Yes. He's at home with Grampa,' Mum said.

Charlie must've been busy elsewhere, because Marco and Phil stayed a good half hour. I was exhausted when they'd finished, trying to remember everything. When the door opened, Phil closed his notebook. But I had more questions. 'You can't go now!'

'Sorry, Martin.' Charlie was in charge again. 'You need to rest.'

Marco stood up. 'The nurse is right, Martin. You've worked hard enough for one morning. Andy Thompson gave us some great info, but you've filled in some more of the gaps. Get some sleep and we'll come back later.'

When they'd left, Charlie felt my forehead and took my pulse. 'Too much excitement for one day,' he said. He turned to my mum. 'Have a break, Mrs Morris. Go and get yourself a coffee. Martin needs a sleep and I'll keep an eye on him for you.'

'I'll be here when you wake up, son.' Mum sounded tired. She paused and her voice wobbled a bit. 'I prayed and prayed last night. Thank God you're safe.' Another memory suddenly came back: *PUSH*. I looked at my arms, but the yellow wristband had gone. And the horrid orange one too. A hospital one was there instead.

'Bye,' I said softly as the door clicked shut. For some stupid reason, a tear trickled on to my pillow. 'Idiot,' I thought. But it kind of felt OK to cry. After all, no one could see me, could they?

Chapter thirteen

When Marco and Phil came back, it was like fitting pieces of a jigsaw together. Fuller, Joe, 'Ansome and the man with no lips had been arrested. 'Good job we know you were set up, Martin, else we'd be rounding you up too: wearing an orange wristband like the rest of them!'

'What's happened to Joe?' I asked.

'Joe's being taken care of alright. And he certainly won't be coming anywhere near you again. As a very wise person once said, "What a tangled web we weave, when first we practise to deceive."'

I thought of all the times Joe had messed me around, about my rugby shirt and the past few days. Well, the war with Fuller was finally over. And even though I was in hospital, I was most definitely the winner.

'If it hadn't been for you and your circles, Martin,' Marco went on, 'Fuller's gang may have got away with it.'

Circles. What circles? It felt strange, not remembering, like catching something in the corner of your eye, but not quite being able to make it out. 'Just before you lost consciousness, Andy said you were going on about circles, and Joe, and the bank?'

Suddenly everything became clear. I could see Bruno's shattered window and the cracks radiating out from the hole in the centre. 'I know! We were doing pictures of

Main Street in Art. Joe's was rubbish. For some reason, he'd put circles on the Plaza and the bank. Somehow, I must've linked the two when I went down and realised what that was all about. But there's one thing I still don't get, Marco. Why on earth did they want to shoot me?'

Marco's eyes widened, 'You were a brilliant diversion! That thug took a pot shot at you to throw us off the scent. They knew someone would call 999 and the place would be swarming with police. And in the meantime, they could get on with the real job just across the fence without any disturbance at all! Clever, eh?'

Phil nodded, 'They had some nerve. If they'd pulled it off, Martin, they'd have made an absolute fortune. But thanks to you, we went straight next door and arrested the lot of them. They'd worked it out to perfection, and it was only a few minutes before the getaway car turned up.'

So that's why the man with no lips was timing the Bravo! Another piece of the puzzle fell into place.

'But the driver got a surprise when he found us waiting for him!' Marco finished the story. 'We arrested him along with the others, so they were all caught up in their crazy, crazy web.'

Phil laughed. 'And they won't be crawling out for a very long time, thanks to you.'

'Traps always belong to the wise ones,' I murmured.

'What was that?'

'Oh nothing.' I smiled for the first time in hospital.

* * *

It was a week before I was allowed home. I had loads of cards from school, and Mum bought the papers with the story in it, although I wasn't named 'for legal reasons' they said. The TV and the radio wanted to talk to me, but the police wouldn't let them. All part of the legal stuff too, apparently. Shame. I would've liked that.

Eventually, my bandage was taken off and the tubes came out. I had to be careful, as my head was still a bit fuzzy, but Mum said it was swollen with all the fame, so I guessed she wasn't worried any more.

The day I came out of hospital, I was hoping there'd be a party or something, but Mum said the police wanted to keep things quiet. Still, it was great to be home. Becker wouldn't stop pestering me and Grampa wasn't much better. 'You sit by me, boy.' And I was more than happy to snuggle in beside him, like when I was little. Mum made jerk chicken for tea, and we had key lime pie too. 'But I'm only doing it this once!' she said.

After tea, the doorbell went. Mum answered it.

'Andy!' I stood up.

'007! You sit down!' And he gave me a hug. His mum followed with a big box of chocolates. 'It's great to see you looking so well, Martin,' she said. 'God is good.'

My mum smiled at her. 'Let's make a drink,' she said, and they headed off to the kitchen.

Andy fiddled with his sleeve. It was funny seeing someone else stuck for words, so I started to talk instead.

'My wristband went missing. Sorry.'

Andy winked, and reached into his pocket. 'It's a good job I thought of that then.' He handed over a familiar yellow band. 'I guessed they'd take it off you in hospital.'

I put it straight on and took a deep breath. 'Thanks, Andy. When I was waiting in the Plaza, I told God I was sorry for those wrong choices I'd made.' I knew I'd gone red, but I didn't care. 'I think I need to find out some more about him.'

'Wow! That's wonderful,' he smiled. 'Come to 24-7 with me on Monday.'

'I'd like that.'

Grampa snored a bit. We laughed and I opened the chocolates.

'The police came to talk to you, didn't they?' I offered Andy the box.

He took one. 'Yep. They wanted "my version of events", they said.'

'Which was ...?'

'OK.' Andy finished his chocolate. 'I was waiting out on Main Street when Becker started barking. I spotted the man, and straight away I knew he was the one you'd seen before. But then I saw ... the gun.' He went quiet. 'I'm sorry, Martin. I couldn't think what to do, it happened so fast. It was like being in a film—except it was real.'

'It's not your fault,' I said.

'No, but I keep dreaming about it.' He shrugged. 'When that man fired the gun, I realised you were down and I raced into the Plaza. I thought ... I thought you were dying. But you went on about circles and the bank before you passed out. What was that all about?'

I filled Andy in. 'But d'you know what? I still can't think why Fuller would target me,' I finished. Neither could Andy. We took another chocolate and tried to work it out, but when Mum brought the drinks in, we were no further forward.

Chapter fourteen

The last part of the story finally came to light because of Bruno. I wasn't back at school, Grampa was at the day centre and it was just me and Becker at home. Mum was working an early shift so she could come home at lunchtime and keep an eye on me. She was worried about what would happen at the Golden Larches with Leon Fuller 'otherwise occupied' as she put it. Someone from somewhere or other had been brought in to run the place, but it was all a bit up in the air.

Daytime TV was boring. I switched it off, yawned and was thinking about going for a lie down, when the doorbell rang.

'Bruno!' I held on to Becker's collar as he tried to make a run for it. 'How do you know where I live?'

'Oh, I know most things round here!' He smiled. 'Can I come in?'

I took him through to the living room and offered him a drink. 'No thanks. I can't stop long. Liza will be after me with her rolling pin!' I laughed.

We talked about what had happened: the shooting, the window and the gang.

'It's good that Mr Anselm and the others are behind bars, Martin. I told you that God would make sure that justice was done. He is in control, you know.'

'Yes, I do, Bruno. And Marco got his own back in the end!' We laughed.

'And it might change things for your dad too.'

'Pardon?' I tried to keep my voice steady. 'Dad?'

'Well, all those rumours take on a whole new complexion, don't they?' Right then I heard Mum's key in the door. A few minutes later, Bruno had gone.

When we sat down with our sandwiches, Mum chatted away but I wasn't listening. 'Martin! Martin!'

I shook my head. 'Sorry. I was miles away.'

'I can tell. Are you feeling alright? You sure you're OK?'

I took a deep breath. This was my chance—perhaps the only one I'd have. And I took it. 'Mum, can I ask you something? It's important.'

She folded her arms. 'I expect so.'

'Don't get mad at me, will you? When Bruno was here, he mentioned ...' I struggled to get the word out, '... Dad.' I couldn't look at her, and what I said next came out in a rush. 'He mentioned things changing for him with all that's happened?'

Mum sat very still, like she didn't know what to say. When she started to talk, her voice was shaky. 'For what you've been through, Martin, you deserve an honest answer. This past week's been hard, but there's something else too. Your ... father,' she broke off, almost as if she had the same problem as I did in naming him. 'I never told you why he was put away.' There was a long silence. 'He was jailed because of a bank robbery.' I gasped.

'I'm sorry, Martin.' She looked at me properly for the first time. 'I was only trying to protect you by keeping it quiet.' She stopped. And I waited. 'It—it was like this.

We'd been married less than a year when you came along. It was a struggle to make ends meet, your dad lost his job and I was looking after you. We were up to our necks in debt when your dad said he had a friend he could borrow some money from. I begged him not to, but he wouldn't listen. In the end, it went wrong and we ended up owing a fortune. And the man he borrowed from was...' she almost spat the words out, '... detestable, evil, a lowlife.' She stopped. 'And he put the thumbscrews on. "Pay back or else." Your dad was so desperate, he went out, bought a gun from goodness knows where and went for a bank. And it wasn't any old bank.'

'Don't tell me.' Of course I knew. 'The bank on Main Street.'

She nodded. 'Yes. The one next to the Pizza Plaza. And what I haven't told you is who the man was who loaned your dad the money. It was Fuller. Leon Fuller.'

'Fuller?' I shook my head. It couldn't be!

'Yes, Fuller. When he was caught, your dad told me Fuller had set him up, but I really thought he was stupid enough to do it on his own, so I didn't believe him.' She started to cry. 'After last week, though, it looks like he could have been telling the truth.' When she'd pulled herself together, my mum carried on. 'Your dad was put away for four years. That's a long time, and I told him I never wanted him back. So when he was released, he didn't come home.' She found a tissue and twisted it in her hands. 'I thought Leon Fuller was our friend and that he gave me the job at the Larches to help us out. He played on that, always making me feel as though I owed him something—probably to make sure I didn't suspect him. And that's why I made you be friends with Joe. And that's why I wouldn't even let you mention your father. I've ruined your childhood, Martin. Ruined it!' She started sobbing those big hiccup sobs.

I didn't know what to do. 'I'll make us some tea,' I said.

'Thanks, love,' she said when I came back. The mug shook in her hand, but she was calmer after a few sips.

'Mum? I still don't get why Fuller decided to go for the bank again.'

'I'm not sure either, to be honest, but I learnt to play dumb with him a long time ago. I picked up a lot that way.'

I half smiled. 'We Morrises are good at that, aren't we?'

'I have a theory, though,' she carried on. 'The Larches was definitely golden when it started out—a nice little goldmine—but it didn't stay that way. Fuller was losing money hand over fist, and I know things were getting really bad. So maybe that's why he went back.'

'OK. But how did I get caught up in it?'

Mum blew her nose. 'I've been thinking about that too. At work, Fuller couldn't stop making comments about your dad being a lousy bank robber. He must've hated him for messing up his plot and it really wound him up—even ten years on. "My Joe could have done better. A *real* man could do it standing on his head." I couldn't work out why he kept going on about it, but I can now.' She paused and looked up. 'Do you know what I think, Martin? Fuller decided to target you as a sick way of finally closing that chapter on your dad—a chapter that I'd read all wrong. That's why I needed to show you how much I loved you when I nearly lost you.'

She started to cry again, and I gave her a hug. 'But it didn't work, did it, Mum?' I said softly. As she clung on to me, I thought of Andy's wristband. In all that had happened, I'd made a brilliant choice. I'd proved I could rely on God one hundred per cent. 'I'm going to be OK.' She pulled back and smiled.

There was only one question that still needed clearing up. 'So where does all this leave Dad?'

Mum sat back. 'Your father *was* in the wrong,' she said. 'He was armed, and almost got away with it, and he paid well and truly. Four years inside and he lost his family. But it's not right that he took Fuller's punishment as well.'

Lots of things were coming together in my head, and I started to say them out loud, more to myself than Mum. 'Andy said he hated seeing me taking the rap for Joe. And Dad did the same for Leon Fuller. But that's what Jesus did: he took the rap for us when he'd done nothing wrong. Makes you think, doesn't it?'

Mum nodded, and I suddenly knew what I had to say. 'It's scary, Mum, but you must tell someone. You can't leave it.'

'I know Martin. I've known all along.' She finished her tea, looked up the number and dialled the local police station.

Chapter fifteen

It was a few weeks later when we saw my dad. We agreed to meet at the Plaza on a Saturday—'Keep it neutral,' Mum said. The table was booked for six thirty; after all, it was usually quiet then. I clipped Becker to the railings while Mum went inside with Grampa. It felt weird: like I'd done all this before. And, of course, I had.

I played with Becker's lead to buy some time. Mum needed to see Dad first. And the shy me had come back. I looked across the road for a moment and shivered, but there was nothing out of the ordinary, only a pair of magpies pecking at something in the gutter. 'Good boy. No barking tonight!' I patted Becker and he settled down. Then I opened the Plaza door.

'Hi Bruno. Is that another song for me?'

Bruno laughed and rubbed his arms, '"Crazy"! That'll be me if you don't shut the door. Crazy with cold! Your folks are down the far end, right away from that window.'

I went to join them, then hesitated. The man didn't look like how I remembered my dad. He was smart and clean and tidy, his hair greying at the sides. Mum was crying and I didn't know where to look. I pulled my sleeves down over my hands and played with the cuffs. I studied the pictures of Italy on the walls, the fake lemon tree, the plant by the till, the tips bowl, the little towers of Pisa.

'Go on,' Bruno whispered. 'It's OK.'

'Martin?'

I stepped forward, my heart thudding in my chest. 'Dad?'

Our pizza was good, and Grampa even managed some lasagne. When we'd finished, Dad told us how sorry he was. No one knew what to say. Mum fidgeted, Dad started to make a boat out of his serviette and I looked everywhere but at Mum and Dad. And it was then that I noticed it.

'Dad. What's that?'

He rolled up his sleeve. 'This?' he said, playing with a black band on his wrist.

It didn't say *FROG* or *PUSH*, and I was a bit disappointed. 'Doesn't matter,' I said.

'This means something really special to me,' he said. 'Shall I tell you why?'

I shrugged. I wasn't that interested any more, but he carried on anyway. 'There's four things on it. First, there's a heart. That means God loves me.' I sat up. 'Followed by two crosses. The first one's an *X*, and it means I've done wrong, but the next one means—'

I couldn't wait any longer. 'Jesus died?'

'You know?'

'And the question mark?' I wasn't sure about that.

'That means "So what am I going to do about it?" He glanced at my mum. She didn't say anything, so he carried on. 'You see, Martin, when I was inside, I discovered that was the most important question. So I had a choice to make. And I made the right one.'

I rolled up my sleeve. '*PUSH*,' I said.

Dad's eyes went all shiny. 'That's amazing!' And I knew right there we had the chance of a new beginning.

Bruno brought Mum and Dad their coffees and I had some ice cream. As we were finishing, Grampa spoke up. 'It's so good to be together again,' he said. 'I don't know what's ahead, but I'd like to tell you a story, made especially for tonight.'

Dad winked at Mum and she smiled. 'That takes me back. Go on, Grampa S. Which one?'

Grampa spread his hands on the table. He stared at them for a moment. Then he looked up. 'Where I come from, there's a spider called Anancy ...'

Also available

THE SECRET OF THE HIDDEN TUNNEL

Mary Weeks Millard

Matty Morris's world collapses when her parents announce that they are going to move to Africa and that she will need to go to boarding school. She is sure she won't like St Anne's, but she quickly settles in and makes friends. Through a series of adventures and personal challenges she and her friends make exciting discoveries about the school's history as well as some life-changing decisions ...

Mary Weeks Millard used to work as a missionary in Africa. She now loves to write stories for younger readers.

Also available

S.O.S. TITANIC

Jill Silverthorne

Chrissie and Luke Barwell are surprised to find themselves invited on a trip to America by an aunt they scarcely know. Their journey promises more than they expect when they secure a passage on the White Star Line's newest ocean-going liner. Chrissie, though, is uncertain from the beginning about what the trip may hold.

Based on events of April 1912, the journey turns out to be much more significant than any of the travellers could imagine. How will they cope with the life and death situations they face?

Jill Silverthorne was born and bred in South Wales and it was there she committed her life to Christ. She graduated from the University of Leicester with a degree in English and went on to teach at a sixth form college, before leading a faculty and then becoming deputy headteacher in a secondary school in the Midlands. Jill has always loved working with young people in her job and in church settings. She enjoys preparing youth-based resources for holiday clubs, camps and church youth groups. She has been published in association with her work and also worked with several Christian organisations, writing resources for ministries to teenagers. Jill has a passion to see high quality Christian literature written for young people in the twenty first century. This is her first contribution towards seeing that aim fulfilled.

Also available

RICHES IN ROMANIA

Rebecca Parkinson

Jenny's parents have always been able to give her everything she wants until her dad begins a new job working for a Christian charity. As Jenny struggles to come to terms with their new lifestyle, her family is invited to take part in a farming project in Romania. As Jenny and her brother David spend time in a small Romanian village, they make friends with the local children and begin to realise that friendship can break down barriers of wealth, language and culture. However, when Jenny's precious locket goes missing it seems that everything has gone wrong, until a guard, previously in the Communist regime, teaches her the secret of forgiveness and encourages her to set about putting things right in her own life.

Rebecca Parkinson lives in Lancashire with her husband and their two children. As a teacher and the leader of the youth and children's team in her church, she loves to pass the Bible stories on to others in a way that everyone can understand.

94